GLADIATOR BOY

STOWAWAY SLAVES

Other Gladiator Boy *titles to collect:*

GLADIATOR BOY

STOWAWAY SLAVES

DAVID GRIMSTONE
ILLUSTRATED BY JAMES DE LA RUE

GROSSET & DUNLAP
An Imprint of Penguin Group (USA) Inc.

GROSSET & DUNLAP
Published by the Penguin Group
Penguin Group (USA) Inc., 375 Hudson Street, New York, New York 10014, USA
Penguin Group (Canada), 90 Eglinton Avenue East, Suite 700,
Toronto, Ontario M4P 2Y3, Canada
(a division of Pearson Penguin Canada Inc.)
Penguin Books Ltd., 80 Strand, London WC2R 0RL, England
Penguin Group Ireland, 25 St. Stephen's Green, Dublin 2, Ireland
(a division of Penguin Books Ltd.)
Penguin Group (Australia), 250 Camberwell Road, Camberwell, Victoria 3124, Australia
(a division of Pearson Australia Group Pty. Ltd.)
Penguin Books India Pvt. Ltd., 11 Community Centre, Panchsheel Park,
New Delhi—110 017, India
Penguin Group (NZ), 67 Apollo Drive, Rosedale, North Shore 0632, New Zealand
(a division of Pearson New Zealand Ltd.)
Penguin Books (South Africa) (Pty.) Ltd., 24 Sturdee Avenue,
Rosebank, Johannesburg 2196, South Africa

Penguin Books Ltd., Registered Offices: 80 Strand, London WC2R 0RL, England

Text copyright © 2009 David Grimstone. Illustrations copyright © 2009 James de la Rue.
Published in Great Britain in 2009 by Hachette UK. First published in the United States
in 2010 by Grosset & Dunlap, a division of Penguin Young Readers Group, 345 Hudson
Street, New York, New York 10014. GROSSET & DUNLAP is a trademark of Penguin
Group (USA) Inc. Printed in the U.S.A.

Library of Congress Cataloging-in-Publication Data is available.

ISBN 978-0-448-45420-7   10 9 8 7 6 5 4 3 2 1

For Chiara Stone, my beautiful wife.

ANCIENT ITALY

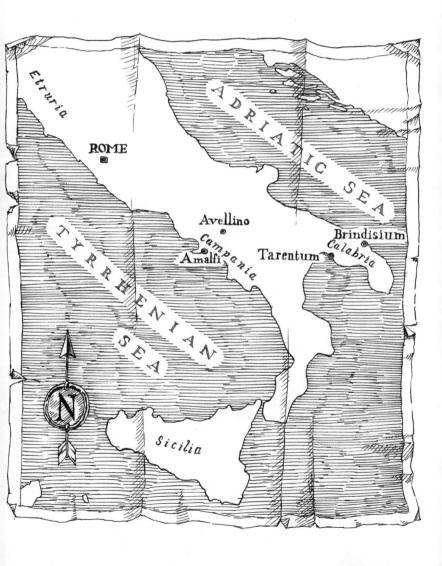

CONTENTS

PREVIOUSLY IN *GLADIATOR BOY*

Decimus Rex has escaped Arena Primus in the company of a fellow slave, Olu Umbika. Together, the pair have managed to do what no one else has ever done—flee the clutches of Slavious Doom. However, with the overlord's evil servant in pursuit of them, it seems only a matter of time before they are recaptured.

CHAPTER I

THE ESCAPE

Slavious Doom was well-known in Avellino, and not simply because his arena loomed over the little town like an angry giant. The overlord was famous for his cruelty, and there was much evidence of this in the tortured screams that regularly erupted from the arena floor.

Despite these fears, the townsfolk managed to go about their everyday lives, largely ignoring the fiendish activities that took place on their borders.

But now nothing could hide the army of arena guards that marched through the gates of Avellino and began barging their way into people's homes.

All over the town, muscled feet connected

with old doors, splintering weak wood and forcing it away from the frames.

Men, women, and children were thrown aside like rag dolls as the guards, many of them expressionless and moving as though they were being controlled by a particularly ruthless puppet master, overturned tables and chairs. The guards ripped open bedding and ransacked cupboards in their efforts to find the escaped slaves.

Beneath the town, an even more frantic search was taking place . . .

The dogs raced along the tunnel, throwing up foul water all around them as their enormous paws sprang off the sewer floor. Despite all being part of the same pack, they were biting

and clawing one another at every turn . . . and only seemed to concentrate on their goal when the sewer opened up before them.

The guards who were supposed to be handling the dogs were in deep trouble, and they knew it. The pack had broken free soon after they'd entered the tunnels, breaking their leashes and wounding several of the guards in the process. Most of the dogs were deformed by years of savage beatings and the rest were simply deranged. If the escaped children were in the tunnels, they wouldn't survive an encounter with the dogs . . . and the guards had clear instructions from Doom to bring Decimus Rex back alive.

"Down there!" screamed the guard captain, a vein standing out on his neck as he splashed madly through the sewer. "You with the sword—take the opposite tunnel! We need to get those dogs back NOW!"

The guards broke off in different directions as the tortured howls of the dogs echoed in the distance.

"This is crazy," said Olu, trying to cover his nose and mouth to avoid breathing in the tunnel's horrific stench. "We're going to get caught and thrown into the dungeon like all the others. We'll never be heard from again!"

"Nah," said Decimus, turning to Olu with a wide smile on his face. "The aqueduct is the LAST place they'll look. It would be different if we'd gone missing INSIDE the arena, but we didn't. They KNOW we scaled the wall, so they'll be looking outside—they've probably raided half of Avellino by now. When that fails, they'll assume we're miles away! Besides, even if they do follow us down here, they'll never find us— this place is a maze!"

The two slaves hurried along the low tunnel, trying to keep to one side to avoid splashing

through the sludgy mix of filth and foul-smelling water that rushed beneath them.

After a few seconds, Decimus stopped and threw back a hand to block Olu from overtaking him.

"What is it?" said the boy, his eyes scanning the tunnel ahead of them.

"A grate," Decimus whispered as voices became audible in the distance. "It's the one we always passed in the tunnel when they led us out."

"And that tunnel is always crawling with guards."

Decimus nodded, and craned his neck to see around the bend in the tunnel. A shaft of light flowed from the grate and penetrated the gloom.

"It's going to be difficult to get around, so we need to choose our moment carefully."

Decimus waited a few more seconds, then crawled around the bend. Olu took a deep breath and followed. By the time he had negotiated the curve in the tunnel, Decimus was already fast approaching the grate and its revealing spear of light. Olu bunched his hands into fists in order to stop them from shaking; when Decimus moved through the light, he was almost afraid to watch. Then, in an instant, it was over . . . and Decimus was on the far side of the grate, beckoning Olu forward with one hand and raising a finger to his lips with the other.

There were voices directly above them, coming from two guards who had evidently avoided being recruited for the hunt but were busy talking about it.

Olu tried to block out their conversation as he crept along beneath them.

"What will Doom do if he finds 'em?" said one. "Do you think he'll just continue the trials as normal?"

"He'll beat 'em both within an inch o' their lives," said the other. "He might even kill 'em, if he's . . . hey . . . what was that?"

Olu froze on the edge of the light stream. As far as he could tell, he hadn't made a sound. Nevertheless, the guards had evidently heard something. He hunkered down in the shadows on the edge of the grate and waited, still shaking with fear. On the far side of the light, Decimus had a troubled, questioning look on his face.

"Look lively," said the first guard, above them. "Someone's coming."

The two guards fell silent as several shadows crossed the grate, blocking out the light as they went. Olu took the opportunity to make a dash for it, using the marching troops as cover. He reached Decimus just as the guards continued their conversation.

"That was Hain's lot, wasn't it? I wonder what they're doing here?"

"I think they've got attack dogs in the sewers. If you ask me, that's risk—"

Decimus and Olu didn't hear the end of the guard's sentence as a sudden splash in the tunnel ahead caused them both to scramble back against the wall.

There, in the distant gloom, was a heavy-set guard. He'd dropped into the sewer through a grate farther along the tunnel and was proceeding toward them.

"Back!" Olu whispered frantically. "We need to go back!"

"No," Decimus shouted, grabbing his friend by the arm and driving him against the sewer wall. "There's at least two guards above that grate!"

As his voice echoed loudly in the tunnel, two things happened at once.

First, the guard in the tunnel ahead spotted them in the shadows and charged forward with a loud cry. Then, the grate above them was wrenched aside, and the two guards dropped into the sewer beside them.

Decimus scrambled backward and slipped into the river of murky water, one hand clamped over his mouth. Olu simply froze where he was standing. Neither of them noticed that the sound of distant howling had grown steadily louder with every passing second.

"You boys stay right where you are," warned the solitary guard, drawing his sword and holding it in front of him.

"I'd listen to him if I were you," echoed one of the two guards behind the boys. "We've got you now; don't make it worse by trying anything . . . foolish."

Decimus gritted his teeth, and in that second Olu knew that his friend was about to do something very, very foolish indeed.

Without a single word of warning, Decimus charged the two guards behind him. In the last split second, however, as they were raising their fists and preparing to tackle him, he suddenly changed direction and barreled headfirst into the guard on the other side of the tunnel. The boy moved with such speed

that his
enemy
was taken
completely
by surprise,
and the pair
crashed to
the floor in a
complicated web of punches and kicks.

The howling in the tunnels reached fever
pitch, and even Olu was distracted from
his fear. He kicked himself away from the
sewer wall and took up a defensive stance,
seemingly inviting the two guards to attack.

Then the situation in the tunnel exploded
into chaos.

At first, Olu thought the guards had both

made a desperate lunge for him. It was only when they crashed into the water that he saw the dogs. They leaped upon the back of each guard, their drooling jaws working madly as they bit into every exposed piece of flesh they could find.

Olu leaped back and, turning on his heels, splashed through the tunnel toward Decimus and the remaining guard. Locking his hands together, he swung around with his elbow and glanced a well aimed blow at the side of the guard's head. The big man, who had managed to overpower Decimus and was attempting to choke the young slave into unconsciousness, yelped as the blow sent a sharp pain through his neck . . . and released his grip. Decimus used the momentary advantage to draw his legs back.

Then, with every ounce of strength he could muster, he drove both feet squarely into the chest of the guard. The heavy brute flew backward, just as a third rabid dog rounded the bend in the tunnel. Olu flung himself flat, plunging into the water as the monstrous animal leaped over him and landed, in a hail of spittle and filth, on the guard's shoulders.

"Go!" Decimus screamed at the top of his voice, snatching up the big man's sword. "Go! Go! Now!"

He and Olu thundered along the tunnel, taking every new passage they could find and trying to put as much distance between them and the hunting party as they could. Every few seconds they would splash to an abrupt halt as one of the savage dogs tore across a passage in front of them. Neither Olu nor Decimus had any doubt that the dogs would tear them limb from limb if their paths crossed.

They ran on, left, right, ahead, right again.

"Rats!" Olu cried, pointing to an army of giant vermin that spilled out from a junction up

ahead. "Look at the size of them!"
He collapsed against the wall and,
fighting to catch his breath, he
whispered, "Which way should we go?"

"They're both dark and they both stink to
the heavens," said Decimus. "Which way did
those rats come from?"

"The passage on the left. Why?"

"Rats go to the surface for food.
We were always seeing them around the
entrance, don't you remember?"

Olu nodded. "Left it is, then."

The two slaves peered into the new
passage, and then began to crawl into the
gloom. They hadn't taken more than a
few steps, however, when a pair of bright,
demented eyes flashed in front of them.

Pawing slowly out of the shadows, the dog snarled deeply, a low and guttural rasp that grew in pitch as it emerged into the meager light of the junction.

Decimus raised the sword and, to Olu's astonishment, started to growl back. He also, very carefully, turned the sword around so that the blade was facing down, toward his feet and away from the animal.

"What are you doing?" said the stunned slave, taking several steps toward the junction. "Have you gone mad? What—"

Decimus curled his lips so that his teeth and gums were bared. Then he drew in a deep breath and blew a powerful burst of air through his teeth, spraying saliva over the animal as the noise intensified.

"That will make it madder, you idiot!"

"Grrrrraaaaaaargh," Decimus continued. "Grraaargghhh!"

Olu knew the dog was going to leap before it happened, but it soon became apparent that Decimus knew it, too. Instead of diving aside or attempting to dodge the enraged animal, the slave stood his ground and only made his move at the moment when Olu was sure he was doomed.

Gripping the sword tightly in both hands, Decimus brought the pommel up with such ferocity that Olu heard the sickening crack inside his head seconds before he actually heard it in reality.

The pommel slammed into the drooling animal's jaw and it dropped to the ground, hitting the water with a loud splash.

"Now we run," Decimus whispered to Olu. "And we don't stop running until we both collapse."

CHAPTER
II

THE
WRATH

Drin Hain strode along the corridor, his black robes billowing out behind him. Slavious Doom's shadowy apprentice reminded many of the guards who served him of a dark shadow, a hungry ghost who appeared on the battlements of abandoned castles, half demented and hungry for blood. An aura of icy calm surrounded him, and at times it seemed as though he could actually smell the fear in those he chose to question.

Today's unfortunate victim was a jailer named Truli. The man cowered before Hain, his eyes focused firmly on one of the figure's narrow shoulders. It was rumored in the arena that Hain had been horribly burned as a child, and the sight of his face was something

that, once seen, no man could ever forget.
Truli was incredibly grateful that the hood
concealed much of what lay within.

"Your ineptitude has allowed these slaves
to escape," said the rasping voice. "Therefore,
you will seek to avoid a painful death by
following my every command WITHOUT
question. Do you understand?"

Truli bowed his head.

"Anything you wish, I will do gladly," he
whispered. "In the name and glorious mercy
of our lord and master, the great Slavious
Doo—"

"Take me to the dungeons."

Truli quickly leaped to his feet and
plucked a ring of keys from his belt.

"This way, Master," he said. "Where

would you like to start? The cells are divided int—"

"Not the cells, Truli . . . the DUNGEONS. Beneath the arena."

"Y-yes, sir." Truli moved off in an awkward series of limps, but seemed almost hesitant to comply with the orders. "A v-very unusual request, Master. I was always told NEVER to take people down to the—"

"Your orders have changed."

The jailer didn't say another word. Reaching the end of the corridor, he used his keys to open a vast iron portal that seemed to consist almost entirely of locks, bolts, and chains. Eventually, the door was opened and Truli disappeared into the

smoky depths beyond. Drin Hain dismissed
his personal guards and followed the jailer
down. The corridors below were dank but
extremely well lit, with mounted braziers
positioned at regular intervals on the ancient
walls.

The two men walked in silence for a time,
as two flights of steep and dusty steps gave
way to a long, sloping corridor that itself
led into yet another subterranean stairwell.

37

Eventually, the moans and wails of various tormented souls indicated that they were drawing near the dungeons.

Soon, the passage opened into a vast circular cave with several ropes hanging down from a pulley mechanism that sprouted from the ceiling. The ropes were attached to the floor, which itself appeared to be a giant disc of grated iron.

"Here we are, Master. The Oubliette. This

is where the current crop of failures are."

Hain folded his arms. "Open it."

Several cries rang out from below as Truli
moved over to a rusty-looking crank handle
that stood in front of the wall and began
to turn it in slow, deliberate circles. The
ropes sprang to life, and the disc began, very
slowly, to move.

Hain waited until the pit was half revealed
before he made for the edge. There, glaring

down at a horde of frightened, disturbed, and half-despairing faces, he reached into his robe and produced a roll of battered parchment. As he did so, several of the boys cried out for mercy.

"You will be silent or I will command my guards to pour boiling tar down onto you," Hain snapped. "You will also listen to me VERY carefully. I am about to read out several names from this list. If your name is called out, you will prepare to climb up from the pit in your chains. Then you will follow me. Those whose names are not called will remain—any attempt to escape will be met with death dealt swiftly by my hand. Anyone who doesn't fully understand my words can KEEP ON SHOUTING."

Silence descended on the Oubliette; scores of hopeful eyes turned upward.

Drin Hain unfurled the parchment and, to Truli's surprise, ordered a ladder to be lowered into the pit. Then he began to read out the names.

Several minutes later, a line of four boys was dragged through the dungeon catacombs. Each was connected to the others by a stout chain, so when one staggered and fell, they were all pulled to the ground.

Drin Hain marched along ahead of the slaves, occasionally barking orders or requesting directions from Jailer Truli, who knew the maze of tunnels better than anyone else.

When the group was finally clear of the dungeons and had emerged into the weak sunlight of the arena floor, Hain instructed his own guards to take over for Truli, and the boys found themselves led into a part of the arena they were not at all familiar with. Several flights of stairs dropped away beneath them and, finally, they arrived at a grand doorway that overlooked most of the arena's vast interior. Two sentry guards stood on duty outside.

Hain announced himself to one of the men, who nodded and led the group into a large and ornately decorated room. Plush, red curtains hung from golden rails and several statues occupied the floor space between the door and a raised dais that supported a great arched throne. Upon the throne sat a man the slaves recognized immediately.

Slavious Doom was an imposing figure, his dark hair and beard framing a face that never looked anything less than pure evil. He didn't get up from the throne when the slaves were paraded before him.

"Drin?" he said, an inquiring expression on his face. "What is the meaning of all this? Unless I am very much mistaken, these are NOT the escaped slaves I ordered you to find . . ."

Hain inclined his head slightly.

"Kicking down doors and raiding houses are jobs for brainless servants, my lord.

Your guards have already been dispatched to search Avellino. In fact, I understand the slaves evaded them in the sewers beneath the town. They are faster and smarter than we suspected, and will be halfway across Campania in a matter of days. My time is better spent elsewhere . . ."

He turned to indicate the line of boys beside him, some of whom were barely able to stand.

"On your left, my lord, we have Ruma the Etrurian and Argon the Gaul. Then we have

Teo and, on your right, Gladius the Calabrian. My spies inside the arena inform me that these slaves were all close companions of Decimus Rex and the boy Olu. They were seen talking together during the trials, and they all shared a section in the holding cells."

Doom's expression remained cold. "And?" he snapped. "What of it?"

"My plan is to announce the execution of these boys, at a memorable location, with a second announcement that their fates can be altered if Decimus and his friend hand themselves in to our guard patrols. The Suvius Tower will be a good, strong location, as it is visible for miles around. We can stage the executions there, but also lie in wait for the young . . . heroes."

As a wave of comprehending horror washed over the gathered slaves and they began to dart terrified glances at one another, Drin Hain continued to outline his plan.

"I have it on good authority that the Calabrian was closest to Decimus during the trials. Therefore, his execution alone should bring Decimus out of hiding; the others will be . . . a bonus entertainment. I take it that all of these children are expendable, my lord?"

A sick smile spread across Doom's sharp features.

"They are indeed, Drin," he said. "They are indeed. Your thinking, as always, is inspired. You may proceed with your plan."

CHAPTER III

THE HARBOR

Decimus and Olu had been traveling through the aqueducts for three days, feeding on the sort of scraps that even the rats wouldn't touch and sleeping beside rivers filled with the foulest stench imaginable. At one point they had come upon a vast network of different tunnels but, without the slightest clue as to which way they should travel, they ended up selecting their path largely at random.

However, finally, it seemed that they had hit a lucky break.

"It's a harbor," said Olu, squeezing his face against the bars of the wall-mounted grate they had found. "I can see five, six, maybe even seven ships! We can escape, we can get

away from Doom! Ha-ha! This is
fantastic!"

"I agree," Decimus muttered. "The only problem is that we don't actually have the first idea about where we are. Those ships could be going ANYWHERE!"

"So?" Olu looked amazed at his friend's attitude. "Anywhere is better than the arena, surely?"

"I want to go home, Olu . . . and considering that my home is in Tarentum, there's a good chance we're going in exactly the WRONG direction."

Olu turned to face his friend. His expression was stern.

"You can't go home, Decimus. Not now; probably not ever. Our parents got us into

49

this, remember? Your trials are paying for your father's debts. Don't you think Doom's warriors are likely to be keeping a constant watch on your hometown? Going back to Tarentum right now is just unthinkable. We need to get as far away from Doom as possible. We must get beyond his reach."

Decimus fought back the urge to argue; he knew deep down that Olu was right. There really was no going back home—at least, not yet.

Returning his attention to the grate, Decimus put his hand around the bars and beckoned for Olu to do the same.

"Do you think we can wrench this off?" he muttered. "I think it would be better to go now, in the darkness, than to wait until morning light. The entire harbor will probably be crawling with merchants by then."

Olu nodded, closed his own fists around the grate, and gave it an experimental tug.

"It feels pretty sturdy to me," he admitted. "Let's both pull on the count of three. One, two, three, GO!"

The two slaves pulled on the bars with all their might, but the grate didn't give an inch.

"We need to find another way out," Decimus muttered. "There's no other choice. We'll just have to go back to the last set of steps we passed and up through the opening beside that caved in section of tunnel."

"Yeah, but we can't—that would take us right onto the streets . . ."

"So? We'll have to brave them."

Olu spun around.

"Are you crazy?" he gasped. "We'll be spotted in minutes!"

"Do you have a better idea? Besides, it's

dark outside—that should give us half a chance. C'mon!"

It was dark in the coastal town of Formiae, and a gentle breeze was blowing. The guard patrols on these narrow streets were few and far between, partly because there was seldom any trouble that the locals couldn't sort out, but mostly because even the most dedicated watchmen could be persuaded from their duties by the sounds of merriment. Moreover, the kind of fights that started in harbor towns between rowdy sailors soon turned into large-scale brawls that most common guards would do anything to avoid if at all possible.

Decimus and Olu had been watching a particularly loud and obnoxious pair for the better part of an hour. Their duties seemed to consist of walking up and down the main harbor stretch, glancing occasionally at the line of mostly unmanned ships, and then taking a ten-minute break.

"They're back," Olu whispered, pointing to a doorway some distance from their hiding place in the garden of a small temple overlooking the harbor. "As soon as they get 'distracted' again, we can make our move . . . hang on, they're going inside."

"Right," said Decimus, but he wasn't really paying attention to the guards. His eyes were fixed on the long shadows being cast by the impressive collection of ships that dominated the harbor before them.

"I wish I knew where we were," he muttered.

Olu hadn't taken his own eyes from the lighted doorway.

"We're somewhere on the border of Latium," he said.

"What?" Decimus turned to his friend, visibly shocked at the revelation. "How can you possibly know that?"

"I don't," Olu admitted. "I'm guessing, but I've been to Latium before—a place called Caieta—and the guard's armor was very similar. I bet we crossed the border between Campania and Latium while we were in the aqueduct. Decimus..."

Olu reached over and slapped the young slave on the shoulder.

"What?"

"They've gone back in. Time for us to move!"

The two friends detached themselves from the temple garden and began to run for the nearest ship, ducking and rolling several times when a doorway opened and a party of rowdy sailors spilled out.

Scrabbling in the dirt, Olu managed to drag himself behind a small collection of barrels mere seconds before one of the sailors made a loud and worrisome remark to his companions.

"What was that?"

Three of the revelers continued to stagger toward the next inn, but one wandered over to join his swaying mate.

"I heard something; I think I saw something, too."

Olu tried to peer out from his new hiding place without attracting any attention, but he couldn't see Decimus anywhere. *Still*, he thought, *with any luck those two sailors can't see him, either.*

"Thieves, I'll bet, tryin' to get on a ship."

The first sailor began to lurch in Olu's direction. His companion tried to do the same, but quickly collapsed into the dirt. As Olu slowly moved himself even farther behind the barrels, he saw the sailor flop about in the dirt and attempt to get up several times before he finally passed out.

Unfortunately, the same could not be said for the first, who was advancing on Olu's position with surprising speed, and now seemed to be armed with a short sword. He had to get away.

Olu leaped to his feet and ran, but he stumbled across a barrel that had fallen over behind the others and crashed to the ground in a heap. The sailor was on him in seconds.

"You there! Hold up, thief!"

The sailor charged forward, but Decimus emerged from the shadows, clearing the barrels in one swift jump and landing heavily on the big man's back. Olu looked on in horror as Decimus snatched the sailor's head and twisted it with all his might. The sword clattered to the ground, and the sailor hit the dirt with a dull thud.

"W-what-what—"

"You'd have preferred he ran you through with his blade?" Decimus snapped. "Now come on, we need to move him before that other one wakes up, and then we must get on a ship! There's no time for shock, do you hear me? There's no TIME!"

Olu raced after his friend, the scene playing over and over in his mind. He couldn't

believe how strong Decimus had grown since they'd met on the first day at the arena. Evidently, the numerous trials, battles, and ferocious combats had turned his friend into a formidable warrior. Together, they headed for the nearest ship, dragging the body of the sailor along with them and trying to keep to the shadows.

"Leave him there," Olu whispered as he and Decimus deposited their victim behind an untidy heap of tangled fishing nets. "With any luck, they won't find him until morning."

Decimus nodded, returning his attention to the ships in the harbor.

"The third ship," he said. "That's the one we need to get on. I was watching them all from the temple garden, and the others have skeleton crews still manning them. I haven't seen any movement on the third one at all."

"What type of ship is it?" Olu wondered aloud, squinting at the distant shape. "I'm useless at ships. Don't know the first thing about them."

"Me neither," Decimus admitted. "But it doesn't really matter—the only thing that matters is whether or not we get discovered on board. So let's find ourselves a good hiding place."

"You can try, boys," said a voice behind them. "But not before we've handed you in to the guards and made some nice Denarii."

Decimus and Olu both turned very slowly, but they couldn't see anyone around them. A grim silence settled in the shadows as the two slaves looked left and right, down at their feet and, finally, up at the ship that was outlined above them. Unfortunately, they saw the two smiling pirates leaning over the deck of the ship too late to avoid the net that was quickly dropped on top of them.

Olu struggled wildly with the heavy ropes, but Decimus knew enough about fishing nets to know that struggling would just get them more entangled, so he relaxed and quickly urged Olu to do the same.

A few seconds later, the pirates were standing beside them, their eyes reflecting the gleam of coins they could already imagine filling their pockets.

"Up," said the first pirate, dragging Decimus and Olu onto their feet. "Me and me mate here will share your reward money . . . the others'll be sorry they went ashore when they see what they missed out on."

"Slump down," Decimus whispered to Olu. "Make yourself as heavy as possible—dead weight! Dead weight!"

The first pirate soon realized he didn't have the strength to lift the net and both boys together, so he motioned to his companion to help. Combining their efforts, they managed to drag the pair upright, but not before Decimus had used the delay to loop one square in his own part of the net over the giant mooring ring that tethered the boat to the harbor.

"Move!"

The pirates dragged Decimus and Olu forward, but soon realized that they couldn't progress any farther than a few feet. The larger of the two men immediately assumed that Decimus was holding himself back; he reached through the net and grasped the young slave by his throat, shaking him vigorously before moving on to Olu and repeating the action.

"NOW MOVE YOURSELVES!" he boomed as the other pirate joined him in a renewed effort to drag them away.

Again, the boys staggered a short distance before coming to an abrupt and immovable halt.

"Net must be snagged on something," said the first, but as he went back to investigate, Decimus grabbed his arm through the net and threw all his weight into the man. Sensing the point of the attack, Olu charged into his friend's back, giving the young slave enough momentum to drive the pirate over the edge of the dock. The big man toppled backward and plummeted between the ship and dock, with Decimus and Olu tumbling after him. Realizing that his companion and the highly valuable slaves were all going over the edge, the second pirate dived after them. He grabbed the end of the net and was dragged along for the ride.

The first pirate met a terrible fate; he had fallen onto a pole that jutted from the water.

Decimus and Olu were caught in the net, which was both good and bad news for them. The good news was that Decimus had hooked the net firmly to the mooring ring, so there was no chance of them falling. The bad news was that the second pirate had managed to hang on to the outside of the net, and had produced a dagger, which he was using in an attempt to cut through the ropes.

"Punch him!" Decimus cried at Olu, trying to spur his friend into action. "Shake him off!"

"I can't!" Olu yelled, moving his arm as the pirate's knife blade missed the rope and cut into him. "I can just barely hold on as it is!"

Decimus let go of his side of the net and leaped onto Olu's back. The skinny slave gasped in surprise and fought to hold onto the ropes as Decimus climbed over him and, grasping the net tightly in both hands, drove himself forward and slammed his forehead into the face of the struggling attacker.

A spray of blood flew from the pirate's nose, and he dropped the dagger. This time, however, Olu's reactions were just as quick as those of his friend. The slave reached through the net, caught the dagger, and plunged it into the leg of the pirate.

"Argghhhh! You little—"

He didn't finish the curse; Decimus slammed a fist into his jaw and he fell into the water.

Decimus faltered for a moment and lost his grip on the net, but Olu grabbed hold of him.

"Wh-what now?" the skinny slave whispered.

Decimus took a few seconds to catch his breath.

"We cut ourselves out of here and climb back onto the dock," he muttered. "Then we should try and sneak aboard the third ship, like we planned; I certainly don't want to take on more pirates from *that* crew."

CHAPTER
IV

THE
SUVIUS
TOWER

Argon the Gaul looked down at his bruised, swollen wrists, and winced. A series of ropes, chains, and buckles had taken their toll on his flesh, and they conspired with the scars and burns on his back to form a detailed map of agony.

He looked across at the others, but they all seemed equally pained and exhausted. Teo was picking some dirt from his toenails, Ruma was scratching at one of the walls with a tiny shard of splintered wood, and Gladius was slumped in a corner, scratching his belly and moaning about Decimus and Olu betraying them all.

"Oh shut up, will you?" Argon snapped, struggling to his feet and stomping over to the room's heavily barred window. "I'm sick and tired of hearing about it. They've escaped, okay? Good for them. It's not their fault Slavious Doom's bloodhound has a sick sense of humor—I mean, how could they possibly know he'd do something like this? Besides, you're always changing your mind about Decimus—one minute he's your best friend and the next he's stabbed us all in the back. Make up your mind, will you?"

"Do you really think Hain will execute us?" said Ruma. The Etrurian had been silent for most of the morning, so his words drew immediate glances from Gladius and Teo.

"Of course he will," Argon confirmed. "The man's a monster or a lunatic or worse."

"Yeah," said Gladius, sulkily. "Some of the stories about his brutality have to be made up, though. Surely no one can be THAT bad?"

"You're willing to bet your life, are you?" Argon muttered. "What's left of it, anyway . . ."

Teo stopped picking at his feet and cast a doubtful expression at the Gaul.

"What's wrong with him?" said Argon.

Gladius shrugged. "He probably doesn't understand what's happening."

"Yeah," Argon agreed. "Well, that will change when Hain marches in here and runs us all through with his sword."

Teo suddenly scrambled to his feet and crossed the room in two long strides. Argon stepped back instinctively, but Teo hurried past him and moved to stand beside the window.

". . . Where . . ." he said, pronouncing the word as if it was the most complicated thing he'd ever had to say, ". . . are . . . we . . . ?"

Argon, Ruma, and Gladius all shared glances in the stunned silence. Apart from his name, these were the first words Teo had ever spoken to them.

It was Gladius who answered.

"We're in a place called the Suvius Tower," he said. "It's about five miles from the coast of Campania. They brought us here last night, in the cart with all the chains. Do you remember? Do—"

"Of course he does," Ruma interrupted. "He's foreign; he's not stupid. How do you know where we are, anyway?"

Gladius heaved himself off the dusty floor and padded over to the window. The view was mostly flat land, punctuated in places by the odd town or the outline of a distant city.

"I heard the guards talking when we were in the cart," he continued. "YOU all fell asleep."

"I've heard of the Suvius Tower," said Ruma, a dark expression on his face. "It's a place for . . . big events. People come from miles around to watch."

"By big events you mean executions, right?" Argon spat. "C'mon—at least have the guts to say it."

Ruma glared at him.

"FINE. I was just trying not to dwell on the bad stuff, okay?"

"Whatever," said Gladius, with a dismissive shrug. "We're all doomed, anyway."

The door flew open at that moment, causing all of the gathered slaves to step back very warily.

Three guards entered the room, making way for a short and gaunt-looking jailer who marched in wearing the sort of spiteful expression the boys had come to recognize in many of Doom's servants.

"I have news for you," he said, his words dripping with poisonous undertones. "The great Slavious Doom and his honorable servant Drin Hain have decided that you will each die in an interesting and entertaining manner, for the amusement of his lord's guests. In three days' time . . ."

He looked around the room, his eyes finding Ruma, then Teo, and finally Argon, before they came to rest on Gladius.

"One of you will be thrown from the top of this very tower . . . "

The little jailer allowed his message to sink into the minds of his audience before he continued. "After that, another of you will be dropped into one of several cages. The cages will be covered, so you will not know your fate until it is upon you. We currently have a wonderful selection of lions, snakes, sharks, and crocodiles . . . so, once again, entertainment for Lord Doom's guests will be assured."

All four slaves managed to hold the jailer's gaze, not one of them giving the little man the satisfaction of seeing their fear.

"Then, when only two of you remain, one shall be hung on a scaffold in the square at the base of this very tower. The other . . .," he hesitated slightly, another cruel smile spreading across his face, "will have the honor of being executed in traditional style by the hand of Drin Hain himself . . . in a duel of mortal combat."

The jailer started to laugh, but he was quickly interrupted by Argon.

"Who gets what?" he snapped. "Are we allowed to know which of us will go first?"

The jailer smiled again, his jackal features creasing up so his face was consumed by folds of loose flesh.

"You will all find out at the appointed time . . . and then you will be able to watch one another suffer!"

He turned and went to leave the room, pausing briefly in the doorway and casting a sly glance back at the group.

"Unless your friends give themselves up, of course," he muttered.

Ruma, Argon, Teo, and Gladius watched as the group paraded out of the room and slammed the door behind them. The jailer's cackle still echoed through the tower several minutes after the spiteful little wretch had

departed.

CHAPTER V

HIDING OUT

The ship had departed shortly before dawn. Decimus knew this because there were slivers of light penetrating the hiding place he and Olu had found upon boarding it. Unfortunately, the space behind the captain's cabin soon proved to be a busy spot and so they'd decided to relocate elsewhere. Now they were hunkered down in the bilge, wedged between stinking barrels and chests that smelled like they were full of rotting fish.

"Did you notice those benches on the deck above?" Decimus whispered, pulling Olu away from a potentially noisy rack of chains.

"What?" came the hushed reply. Olu shook himself from his reverie. "Yes, I

saw them . . . and
the oars. This
is a slave ship,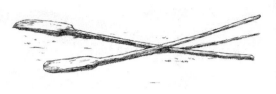
Decimus. You know what that means?"

"Yeah," said the young warrior, with a
grim smile. "It means that if we start trouble
while we're on board, we'll have the slavers
outnumbered."

When Olu looked up sharply, his eyes
wide and his jaw gaping, Decimus quickly
raised a hand.

"Relax, Olu. I know we can't afford to be
captured on here."

The other slave smiled, and a flood of
relief washed over him.

"I'm not like you, Decimus," he said. "I
don't think I can do this much longer. I'm

so very tired, and my bones feel like they're crumbling."

"You're doing well, Olu. Just remember, if it weren't for you, we would never have escaped from the arena. You SAVED us. It's my turn now—whatever we do next, I will make it happen. I just need you to go along with me. Shhh—someone's coming!"

The two slaves crawled deeper into the shadows as a pair of sweaty-looking galley slavers clambered down the steps and began to stalk around the bilge.

"C'mon," said one. "We'd better get this barrel up or the captain will make us row in place o' the slaves . . . like he did last week when old Reeky talked back to him."

"It was hard going, that was," said the other, spitting on the floor and cracking his knuckles. "I don't know how those skinny scrapers manage it."

"They get whipped if they don't row. They get no food if they don't row. They get drowned if they don't row. THAT is how they manage it. Besides, it was hard because there were only eight of us; there's forty of them! We should get to the Suvius Tower with time to spare, I think."

Together they lifted a barrel from the bilge and began to heave it toward the steps. After dropping the load several times, the two slavers eventually managed to get it onto the deck above, and soon scrambled after it. As the second one disappeared through the gap, a scroll fell from his tunic and landed in a puddle of dirty bilge water.

Once the slavers were gone, the shadows seemed to return, creeping around the huddled pair like spears of black mist. The *drip*, *drip*, *drip* of a thousand tiny leaks echoed throughout the bilge.

"Did you hear that?" Decimus whispered. "They're going to trade with Drin Hain . . . and there's only a handful of them! Can you believe that?"

"Don't even think about it," said Olu. "The eight slavers are probably built like Roman fortresses with muscles like granite and the forty slaves are probably all starving skeletons with diseases who lack the will to live. Wait here a second . . . I see something."

Olu crawled around the perimeter of the bilge and crouched beside the steps. Glancing over his shoulder at Decimus, he put a thin finger to his lips. Then he picked up the wet scroll that lay in a small puddle of bilge water beside the hatch and scampered back to where Decimus was hiding.

"One of the slavers dropped it," he panted. "It might be orders or something. I can't read it, though. You'll have to tell me what it says."

Decimus rolled his eyes and began to scan the parchment. Even in the shadows, Olu saw the look of horror slowly consume his friend's tired face. The young slave swallowed a few times, but didn't reply. He looked up at Olu, then down at the scroll once again.

"What IS it? Tell me!" urged Olu.

Decimus stretched the scroll to its full length, and glared at the words that were burning into his eyes as they followed each line of text.

"It's a notice," he said aloud. "It says: *News on escaped slaves, Decimus Rex and Olu Umbika.* There's a description of us both; pretty accurate, I'd say."

Olu nodded gloomily. "Doom has a reputation,"

he said. "He and Hain will NEVER stop looking for us. They'll track us down until—"

"Listen to this," said Decimus with a grimace. "*To ensure the full attention of the two slaves, we have arranged a series of four private executions for the night of the 24th at the Suvius Tower in Southern Campania. Those scheduled for execution are the cellmates of Decimus Rex and Olu Umbika. The executions will only be canceled if their friends hand themselves in to us. Should this fail to occur, we can guarantee a night of brutal entertainment for those with money and a taste for violence. Price of entry: one hundred Denarii.*"

Olu remained silent for a long time. It was Decimus who managed to speak first.

"We can't let this happen," he said. "The 24th is tomorrow night, by my calculation.

They're doing this because of us! Gladius, Argon, Ruma, Teo. They're all going to suffer and die because we escaped."

Olu shook his head. "It's a plan to draw us out! Surely you can see that?"

"It doesn't matter!" Decimus snapped. "Whether it's a plan or not, we both know Doom and his twisted servant will go through with it! They don't CARE about Gladius, or Ruma, or any of them. You don't have to go back, Olu . . . but I must. I wouldn't have gotten through half of those trials if it wasn't for Gladius and the others. I can't let them die for me, Olu. I just can't."

Olu shook his head sadly. "You really think they would do the same for you if the situation were reversed?"

Decimus shrugged. "That doesn't matter—I can only think for myself, not for others. I was told that a long time ago, and it's true. Whether they could leave me to my death is for them to decide should they ever need to—but right now, the decision is mine."

Olu nodded and lowered his head. For a long time, Decimus was afraid his exhausted friend might burst into tears or simply curl up and sleep. Eventually, however, the slave raised his head once again, and Decimus spotted the familiar look of deep, determined thought on Olu's weathered face.

"Then we go back in force," he muttered, gritting his teeth. "The Suvius Tower is on a rock that juts out over the coast. If this ship has been there before, we have the perfect weapon. Hain's slave-traders won't be expecting an attack."

"An attack?" Decimus repeated, wearing a puzzled expression. He almost didn't recognize the boy now standing in front of him as the same tired figure he'd escaped with.

"A major attack," Olu confirmed. "We don't go back and just hand ourselves in—we storm the tower. Of course, we'll need to free the other slaves on this ship." Olu climbed to his feet, using a barrel for support. "To do that, we need a master key to their chains. Then we can take out the slavers and gain control. There were enough swords in the captain's cabin to give everyone on board at least two each." He turned to Decimus, who was looking surprised and impressed by his friend's sudden determination.

"The big question," Olu continued, "is whether or not you think we can lead a horde of mutinous slaves to victory? I wouldn't even think about trying it, myself—but after seeing you in those sewer tunnels, Decimus, I believe you can do anything."

Decimus turned to his friend, but the smile soon drained away from his face. As he peered over Olu's shoulder, a hatch at the other end of the ship was suddenly flung open, and a strangled cry erupted from the deck above . . .

COMING SOON

Slavious Doom has a sick sense of humor and is using Decimus and Olu's friends in a deadly game of cat and mouse. Can the boys capture the slave ship they are hiding on and make it back to the Suvius Tower in time to rescue their friends? The odds are stacked against them. Find out if they make it in . . .

THE REBELS' ASSAULT

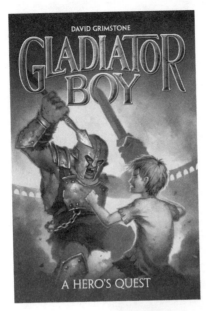

DAVID GRIMSTONE

GLADIATOR BOY

A HERO'S QUEST

DAVID GRIMSTONE

GLADIATOR BOY

ESCAPE FROM EVIL

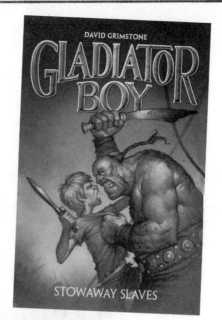

DAVID GRIMSTONE

GLADIATOR BOY

STOWAWAY SLAVES

DAVID GRIMSTONE

GLADIATOR BOY

THE REBELS' ASSAULT

ARENA COMBAT

Get ready to challenge your friends! Each *Gladiator Boy* book will contain a different trial. Collect them all to run your own Arena of Doom—either at home or on the playground.

TRIAL 3
THE HIDDEN

Decimus and Olu spend most of this book in hiding, but how good are you at concealment? This trial is all about hiding things in clever places where no one would think to look.

You will need three players: one to play the shadow-lord Drin Hain and two to play the escaped slaves, Decimus and Olu.

Each hider (the one playing Decimus and the one playing Olu) must select a distinctive stone or pebble and show it to the seeker (Drin Hain). The seeker must close his eyes and turn away from the other players. He must then count to one hundred. While he is counting, the hiders must conceal their objects somewhere nearby.

The seeker then goes in search of the objects, scoring one point for finding one and three points for finding both. He has a time limit of twenty minutes, which can be monitored with a watch.

If the seeker fails to find an item, the player that concealed it receives two points.

Play then revolves until everyone has been Decimus, Olu, and Drin Hain once.

IMPORTANT RULES

The game must be played in a safe place. Players who choose hiding places that are high up or dangerous are immediately disqualified and will score no points for their item remaining unfound. The players must hide their stones within sight of the seeker, meaning that if they were to reveal their items they would be seen immediately. If they go beyond sight of the seeker, their items are disqualified.

The player with the most points at the end of the game is declared the winner!

CHARACTER PROFILE
TEO

NAME: Teo

FROM: The Orient

HEIGHT: 5'5"

BODY TYPE: Slender

BEST FRIEND: Ruma

CELLMATE: Argon

TEO QUIZ: How well do you know Teo? Can you answer the following three questions?

1. WHERE IS TEO WHEN HE IS SEEN PICKING DIRT FROM HIS TOENAILS?

2. WHEN TEO CHARGES AT AN ARCHED WINDOW, WHO THINKS HE IS CHARGING IN FOR A FIGHT?

3. APART FROM HIS NAME, WHAT ARE TEO'S FIRST WORDS?

Answers: 1. the Suvius Tower, page 72; 2. Argon, page 74; 3."Where are we?", pages 74–75.

WEAPON PROFILE: PIRATE WEAPONS

In a previous weapon profile, we looked at various swords. The pirates described in this book would have used something a little different. They would have used a special sort of sword called a *cutlass*.

THE CUTLASS

The cutlass is very similar to a sword, but with one major difference—it has a curved blade. The cutlass was used on many ships because of its ability to cut through thick ropes . . . vital when you're caught in a storm and need to sever the sails!

THE BOARDING AXE

The boarding axe was a special, long-handled axe that pirates used to break down the cabin doors of ships they boarded. There was also another version of the boarding axe: A short-handled one that was used when pirates leaped from one ship to another and slid down the sails, ripping them open as their axes bit through the material. (This latter variety may have existed only in fictional stories and films about pirates, but it's certainly an amazing sight to watch!)

READ MORE OF DECIMUS
REX'S ADVENTURES IN
BOOK FOUR OF THE
GLADIATOR BOY SERIES:

THE REBELS' ASSAULT

Ruma, Argon, Teo, and Gladius were led down from their cell at the top of the Suvius Tower, dragged by the jailer's guards with such force that several cuts and bruises were earned along the way. At one point, Gladius stumbled and fell headfirst down a flight of steps in the tower courtyard. However, rather than stop his momentum, the guards simply laughed and one even gave him an experimental kick to see if he would keep going. By the time the group reached the gates of the fortress, they had stored up enough hatred for their captors to last several lifetimes.

In the courtyard, an eerie silence reigned. The guards assembled the slave line with a series of grunts and shoves. Then they withdrew, making space for the arrival of the spindly, gnomelike jailer who had so gleefully given the prisoners news of their pending executions. He climbed a wooden ladder beside the gates and hurried along a platform that spanned the gap just under the great archway. The slave line followed his progress and their eyes came to rest on the recognizable form of Drin Hain, draped in his trademark black robes and hood. The jailer cupped a hand to his face and whispered something to the ghostlike figure . . .

GLADIATOR BOY

Check out the *Gladiator Boy* website for games, downloads, activities, sneak previews, and lots of fun! You can even get pieces of the arena and fantastic action figures! Sign up for the newsletter to receive exclusive extra content and the opportunity to enter special competitions.

WWW.GLADIATORBOY.COM

LET THE BATTLE COMMENCE!

TO MAKE YOUR OWN ARENA OF DOOM

1. Carefully cut around the outline of the arena section. Ask an adult to help if necessary.
2. Fold across line A. Use a ruler to get a straight edge.
3. Fold across line B. Use a ruler to get a straight edge.
4. Ask an adult to help you score along lines C & D with a pair of sharp scissors.
5. Fold up over line E and push the window out.
6. Repeat instructions 1 to 5 for each Arena of Doom piece collected.
7. Glue the top of each tab and stick them to the next piece of the arena. Repeat as necessary.

CHECK OU
THE WEBSI
FOR A PHOTO
THE COMPL
ARENA.

TO MAKE YOUR ACTION FIGURE

1. Cut around the outline of the figure. Ask an adult to help if necessary.
2. Cut along slot X at the bottom of the figur
3. Cut out Gladiator Boy rectangle.
4. Cut along slot Y.
5. Slide figure into slot Y.

WWW.GLADIATORBOY.COM